baseball's new wave

Andruw Jones

Love That Glove

By
MARK STEWART

THE MILLBROOK PRESS
BROOKFIELD, CONNECTICUT

M

THE MILLBROOK PRESS

Produced by
BITTERSWEET PUBLISHING
John Sammis, President
and
TEAM STEWART, INC.
RESEARCHED AND EDITED BY MIKE KENNEDY
SPECIAL THANKS TO RAY GLIER

Series Design and Electronic Page Makeup by
JAFFE ENTERPRISES
Ron Jaffe

All photos courtesy AP/ Wide World Photos, Inc. except the following:
Andy Lyons/Allsport — Cover
SportsChrome/Rob Tringali, Jr. — Pages 4, 8, 47
Macon Braves Baseball Club — Pages 14, 15
Greenville Braves — Pages 17, 18
The following images are from the collection of Team Stewart:
Topps Chewing Gum — Page 6 (© 1969)
Beckett Publications, Inc. — Page 20 (© 1996)
Red Heart Dog Food — Page 23 (© 1954)
Pinnacle Brands Inc. — Page 29 (© 1996)
Fleer Corp. — Page 30 (©1997)
Century Publishing Company — Page 31 (© 1997)
Dell Publishing Co. — Page 42 (© 1955)

Printed in the United States of America

Published by
The Millbrook Press, Inc.
2 Old New Milford Road
Brookfield, Connecticut   06804

www.millbrookpress.com

Library of Congress Cataloging-in-Publication Data

Stewart, Mark.
    Andruw Jones: love that glove / by Mark Stewart
        p.   cm.   — (Baseball's new wave)
    Includes index.
    ISBN 0-7613-1967-0 (lib. bdg.)
    1. Jones, Andruw, 1977–   —Juvenile literature. 2. Baseball players—United States—Juvenile
literature. [1. Jones, Andruw, 1977– . 2. Baseball players.] I. Title. II. Series.
GV865.J632 S84 2000
796.357'092—dc21
[B]   00-041880

1 3 5 7 9 10 8 6 4 2

Contents

Like Father, Like Son

chapter 1

"Mom, I want to play baseball, just like on TV...so you can watch me every day."

— ANDRUW JONES

When people believe in you, working hard is fun. Henry Jones taught this lesson to his son, Andruw, at an early age. During the 1960s and 1970s, Henry played baseball in Curaçao. And he played it well. In fact, a lot of people thought he was the best player in the tiny island nation, which is located in the Caribbean Sea, about 40 miles (64 kilometers) off the coast of Venezuela.

Because Curaçao is so remote, and because it has a small population, not a single major-league baseball team thought it was worth sending a scout there. That did not matter much to Henry Jones.

As long as the fans cheered and people recognized him in the streets of Willemstad, he was happy to practice hard and play hard. And he was perfectly satisfied to be one of baseball's "best-kept" secrets.

There are few people in the game of baseball who have more to smile about than Andruw Jones. Before he made it to the Atlanta Braves, no one from his country had ever become a major leaguer.

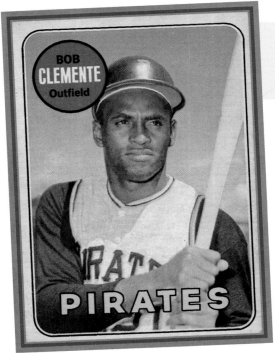

BOB
CLEMENTE
Outfield

PIRATES

Roberto Clemente, the first Caribbean star to make the Hall of Fame. This card was made eight years before Andruw was born.

Andruw was a different story. By the time he began playing ball, the Caribbean had become a treasure trove of talent. Pro teams had scouts everywhere, even in Curaçao. A teenager with a live bat and a strong arm would not remain a secret for long. When word began to spread that there was a 15-year-old who could hit, run, and throw like a young Roberto Clemente, several teams dispatched scouts to evaluate him.

As good as Andruw was, few who saw him back then could have dreamed that he would become a World Series hero before his 20th birthday. And only his closest friends and family knew that he had once *detested* baseball.

Andruw's mother, Carmen, blames his dad for that. Henry Jones was the manager of a plant that made tissue paper. After work, he would rush home to play catch with his two-year-old son. Andruw tried his best, but sometimes he would miss the ball and it would hit him. Hardballs hurt! After a while, Andruw decided it was more fun to "hunt" iguanas. Not until one bit him on the chest did he think about playing baseball again.

By Andruw's sixth birthday, he had fallen in love with his father's game.

Did You Know?

Andruw's name is pronounced "AHN-drew." It is the Dutch spelling of Andrew.

Like a sponge, he soaked up everything his father taught him. Andruw dreamed of making it to the major leagues. Henry Jones still remembers his son singing, "I'm going to play ball in the United States, I'm going to play ball in the United States."

A few yards from the Jones home was a dusty baseball field where kids often played. Andruw played there with his father, and also with his little friends. As soon as he was old enough, he joined a team in the Ant League, which is Curaçao's equivalent of Pee

According to Carmen Jones, baseball fans can thank a backyard iguana like this one for her son's baseball career.

Wee–level baseball. Andruw played everywhere, and rarely needed coaching. His instincts were already very good, and he had the ability to stay calm and clear-headed even in the tensest situations.

When Andruw turned 10, he was invited to join a junior team that traveled to Japan to play in an international tournament. Over the next couple of years, he played more and more often with adults. Finally, he was good enough to be selected for a squad sent to represent Curaçao in the Latin American Games.

As Andruw began his teenage years, his baseball education grew more intense. Henry gave him all of his knowledge, quizzed him on game situations and strategy, and devised training methods to help improve his son's skills. To strengthen his wrists, for example, Andruw would swing a sledge hammer. To increase Andruw's speed, Henry would challenge him to footraces. He would let Andruw get close before pulling away and winning in the last few steps. This forced Andruw to "find" that extra burst of speed when he needed it.

By the age of 15, Andruw was the most complete player in all of Curaçao. He could whip the bat through the hitting zone with tremendous force, and there seemed to be no fly ball he could not run down. Against the modest competition he faced on the island, Andruw simply dominated.

"My dad taught me how to play. He was a great amateur player in Curaçao, and I liked to wear his number whenever I could."

ANDRUW JONES

At about this time, a man named Giovanni Viceisza began hearing stories about Andruw. Viceisza, a businessman who traveled throughout Latin America, was employed part-time by the Atlanta Braves to scout talent in this region. People were always coming up to him, telling him about this kid or that kid. But so many people were talking about Andruw that he figured it was time to check him out. Viceisza went to Puerto Rico, where Andruw was playing in a tournament for Curaçao.

Viceisza was amazed at what he saw. Andruw was not a skinny young boy. He was as big as his teammates, many of whom were 10 years older. He could hit farther, throw harder, field better, and run faster than they could. And he was not playing the game purely on instinct—he clearly knew what to do in almost any situation. Excited, Viceisza contacted the Braves and encouraged them to send a senior scout to see Andruw.

A few days later, Paul Snyder, an astute and experienced judge of talent, was in Curaçao to get a look at the island's best player. He watched as Andruw effortlessly tracked down balls in the outfield, gunned throws to all bases, and crashed home run after home run in batting practice.

Also at this tryout was Andruw's father. When Snyder pulled out a stopwatch and asked the teenager to run 60 yards (55 meters) as fast as he could, Henry Jones lined up next to him on the starting line. When the signal came, father and son exploded into a full gallop. Just like the old days, Henry pushed Andruw to the limit. But this time, it was the younger Jones who turned on the afterburners and streaked across the finish line first.

Did You Know?

As a boy, Andruw's two best positions were catcher and third base. He switched to the outfield as a teenager.

Snyder looked at his stopwatch in disbelief. What was more amazing? The fact that 15-year-old Andruw had completed the course in 6.73 seconds? Or that 46-year-old Henry had finished in 7.16, just a stride behind?

Quiet and colorful Willemstad, where Henry and Andruw Jones became baseball legends.

When Andruw signed with the Braves, this is how they pictured him—swinging for the fences in a major-league uniform. Not even the most optimistic team officials, however, thought he would progress so quickly.

The Curaçao Comet

chapter 1

"Everything is so much bigger here compared to back home. I like it here."
— ANDRUW JONES

Paul Snyder sent back one of those reports that stay with a scout for the rest of his career. Either he would look like a genius or a bum. Ultimately, that would be up to Andruw, whose dream of playing ball in the United States was about to come true. The Braves would have grabbed him right then and there had it not been for a rule prohibiting major-league teams from signing a player before his 16th birthday.

Over the next several months, other teams heard about Andruw and also showed interest in signing him. But Andruw was determined to be a Brave. Atlanta's games were carried on

Did You Know?

Besides English, Spanish, and Dutch, Andruw speaks Papiamento, the native language of Curaçao.

WTBS, a cable station available in Curaçao. If Andruw made it to the majors, he wanted everyone who cheered for him as a kid to be able to watch him as an adult.

Andruw signed with the Braves because he thought his family and friends would be able to see him on the team's cable station, WTBS.

Andruw's biggest decision was whether to sign right after his 16th birthday or to wait. He was a good student, and his parents hoped he would finish high school. Joining the Braves organization right away would mean leaving school without a diploma. Andruw and his parents discussed this situation. They knew his school, St. Paulus, did not have a baseball team, so if Andruw stayed in Curaçao his development might be slowed. They did not want to kill Andruw's dream.

In the end, they made a deal. Andruw could go to America and play ball. If he did not make it to the majors after a few years, he would return home and complete his education. On July 1, 1993—about ten weeks after he turned 16—Andruw and the Braves made it official. The team handed him a bonus check for $46,000, which Andruw turned over to his parents. He continued to play baseball in Curaçao over the next few months, then packed his bags for the United States. He arrived at his first professional training camp in February 1994 the way most 16-year-olds do—a little tired, a little frightened, and very, very excited.

Actually, Andruw had one big advantage over the other young Spanish-speaking

Did You Know?

Andruw was one of three players at Danville in 1994 who would play a key part in the Atlanta Braves' 1999 National League pennant drive. The other two were pitchers Kevin Millwood (above) and John Rocker (right).

players in camp. As a boy, he had been taught to speak both English and Dutch by his parents. Curaçao is a Dutch colony, and the language is still spoken on the island. Spanish was the language spoken in nearby Venezuela, so he learned that, too. As for English, well, it just made sense to learn that, too—especially if a player planned to become a major leaguer. Knowing English made the transition to life in the United States easy. Whereas the other boys were scared to death, Andruw felt like he was on a great adventure.

For the 1994 season, the Braves started Andruw off with their club in West Palm Beach, Florida. The team struggled to win more than a game a week, and the players' stats were awful. But the main goal at this level is not necessarily to win—it is to identify which players have the "tools" to move higher in the farm system. Andruw was one of many exciting young players at West Palm Beach who improved dramatically over the next few years, including Wes Helms, George Lombard, Fernando Lunar, Bruce Chen, and Micah Bowie.

Despite hitting just .221, Andruw was promoted after only 27 games. He and another 17-year-old, Glenn Williams, joined the Danville Braves of the Appalachian

League at mid-season. By the end of the year, Williams was voted the league's most promising player. Andruw, whose .336 average was just three points short of the league lead, was chosen as the number-two prospect. He was also recognized by *Baseball America* as one of the Top 10 prospects in all of the minor leagues.

One of the fun things for Andruw during his first year was signing autographs. In minor-league parks, the fans and players are never far from one another. While some teammates thought it was a big hassle, Andruw was honored that people wanted his signature. Even today, when he is mobbed in public by autograph hounds, he still does not mind. "It's baseball that I love," he explains, "and this is part of baseball."

Andruw's climb up the minor-league ladder continued in 1995. He spent the year with the Braves' Class-A team in Macon, Georgia. Andruw hit a home run in his very first at bat, and seven more in the next nine games. Less than two weeks into his second pro season, the 18-year-old center fielder was batting .476 with 21 runs batted in.

Did You Know?

BASEBALL WEEKLY caused quite a stir in the spring of 1995 when it previewed the Macon Braves. Andruw was identified as coming from the Netherlands (in Europe)!

The Braves were excited about Andruw's fast start, but they were more interested to see how he would handle the rest of the year. Baseball is an endless game of "cat and mouse." When a hitter gets hot, opponents look for another way to pitch him. When they find it, they stay with it until the batter adjusts. When he does, and he starts hitting again, his opponents find a new way to pitch him. This battle starts in the minor leagues and continues right on up to the major-league level—even superstars must constantly "adjust to the adjustments."

Did You Know?

The last minor leaguer to hit 25 homers, knock in 100 runs and steal 50 bases was Jose Cardenal in 1961.

Andruw did indeed go into a slump. But he quickly learned to lay off the pitches he could not hit, and wait for a good one to come across the plate. When the season ended, he had 25 home runs and 100 RBIs. The Braves were thrilled with Andruw's power surge. They were just as happy with his baserunning. He led the South Atlantic League with 56 stolen bases and 104 runs scored. Andruw knew from his dad that speed wins ball games, so when he was not hitting he could still contribute on the basepaths and in the outfield. That fall, Andruw was honored as the *Baseball America* Minor-League Player of the Year.

"He had the best start I've seen anyone have in this game...there's been times when he looked like a man among boys."

**MACON MANAGER
NELSON NORMAN**

Have Bat, Will Travel

chapter }

*"He did everything you could ask,
and everything you could hope for,
at every level he played."*

—BRAVES' GM JOHN SCHUERHOLZ

When spring training opened in 1996, Andruw Jones was being called baseball's next "five-tool" player. That meant he could hit for power, hit for average, run, field, and throw. One of those tools, however, still needed a lot of sharpening. Andruw could hit a fastball as well as anyone alive. But when pitchers threw him good curve balls and sliders, he was practically helpless.

Experienced batters know how to spot the spin on a ball the instant it leaves a pitcher's hand. If they see it spinning side-to-side, they know it will bend and drop before it reaches home plate. Andruw had not learned to do this yet. When he thought a pitch was coming right down the middle, he would start his mighty swing. But if that pitch curved away from him, he could not stop. The result was a weak grounder or pop-up, or a swinging strike.

Andruw as a Greenville Brave. He wears his father's number 13 around his neck.

In the low minors, pitchers do not throw good breaking pitches. So Andruw was rarely challenged. In 1996, the Braves started him with their Class-A team in Durham, with plans to promote him one level to their Class-AA Greenville club as soon as they felt he was ready to face better pitching. Andruw worked hard at Durham to polish his hitting skills. The record shows that, in half a season, he batted .313 with 17 home runs. He also had nearly as many walks as strikeouts, which is considered a sign that a young hitter is learning patience.

Andruw moved up to Greenville after 66 games. Teams often keep their top pitching prospects at the Class-AA level, so he got to face some really nasty breaking pitches for the first time in his career. The Braves watched Andruw closely so they could jump in and make quick corrections the moment he seemed to be overwhelmed. Yet it was *Andruw* who was doing the overwhelming. In 38 games, he smoked the ball for a .369 average. He seemed to drive home and score a run every day.

Did You Know?

Andruw's super season at Greenville in 1996 was one of the team's lone bright spots. Only one other regular hit .300, and the Braves finished second to last.

Andruw's average was 25 points higher than the league leader's, but he did not stay in the Southern League long enough to qualify for the batting title. After watching him chew up young pitching, the Braves realized it was ridiculous to keep him in Greenville. They promoted him once again, to Class-AAA Richmond, just one step below the major leagues. All Andruw did there was hit .378, with nine extra-base hits in 12 games.

Meanwhile, a few hours south in Atlanta, the Braves were preparing to defend the world championship they had won the year before. The team had it all—power, pitching, and defense—and many fans believed the Braves ranked among the greatest teams of all time. But as always happens during a long season, some "holes" developed that the Braves needed to plug.

Right fielder Dave Justice, who several months earlier had refused to undergo surgery to repair a dislocated shoulder, popped it while swinging at a pitch in May, and was lost for the season. Rookie Jermaine Dye was called up from Richmond and did a good job replacing Justice, but he hurt his knee. By July the Braves had more problems. The team went on a month-long "road trip" because Fulton County Stadium in Atlanta was being used for the Olympics. Living out of suitcases and traveling from one town to the next seemed to take a lot out of the team, and it showed in poor defense, bad baserunning, and lackluster hitting. Only Atlanta's pitching kept them ahead of the pack in the National League's Eastern Division.

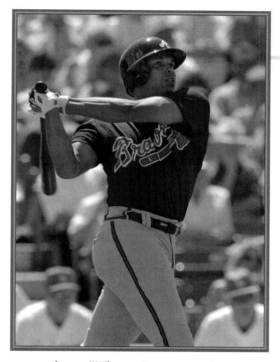

*Dave Justice,
whose season-ending injury
opened the door for Andruw in 1996.*

As Andruw did better and better every time he was promoted, some in the Braves' front office wondered if he might not be a welcome addition to the major-league roster. Andruw was a superb fielder, a fast runner, and an electrifying hitter. With the team's bench players contributing almost nothing, why not bring him up? Just in case that happened, Richmond manager Bill Dancy began playing Andruw in right field—the spot he was most likely to fill if the Braves decided they needed him.

During an August road trip to Norfolk, the team trainer knocked on Andruw's hotel room door. "The trainer came in my room and said, 'Are you ready? You're going to the majors,'" Andruw remembers. "I couldn't speak. I lost my voice!"

minor-league *stats*

Season	Team	Level	G	HR	RBI	SB	AVG
1994	Gulf Coast Braves	Rookie	27	2	10	5	.221
	Danville Braves	Rookie	36	1	16	16	.336
1995	Macon Braves	Class-A	139	25	100	56*	.277
1996	Durham Bulls	Class-A	66	17	43	16	.313
	Greenville Braves	Class-AA	38	12	37	12	.369
	Richmond Braves	Class-AAA	12	5	12	2	.378

* Led League

minor-league *highlights*

Baseball America Minor-League Player of the Year . . . . 1995 & 1996
South Atlantic League Most Valuable Player 1995

JUNE 1996 • ISSUE #62 • U.S. $3.95 CAN $5.50 AUS $6.50

BECKETT.

FS

FUTURE STARS

Teen Phenom
Andruw
Jones

0 74470 84014 5   06

When BECKETT put Andruw on the cover of its June 1996 issue of FUTURE STARS, he was less than two months away from his major-league debut.

Andruw rifles a ninth-inning single against the Philadelphia Phillies for his first major-league hit.

When Andruw arrived in Atlanta, manager Bobby Cox welcomed him to the team and put him right into the lineup. The team needed a spark, he said, and he was counting on Andruw to provide it. On August 15, 1996, Andruw made his major-league debut. He singled home a run against the Phillies and gunned down a runner with a bullet throw from right field. The next day, Andruw hit a home run and a triple. Over the next two weeks, Andruw kept right on hitting and the Braves kept right on winning.

Unfortunately, Andruw's sudden success went to his head. He felt that no one could get him out, and that there was no pitch he could not handle. When the league's veteran hurlers saw this, they started throwing Andruw a lot of junk. Andruw continued to hack away, and in no time, his average dropped and he found himself back on the bench. For the rest of the season, he sat, watched, listened, and learned. He also ended the year in a 1-for-22 slump. When the Braves had to decide whom to keep on the team for the playoffs, Andruw was nearly left off. Only his speed and defense earned him a spot on the postseason roster. That was fine with him. "Defense is what I'm best at doing," Andruw says.

Andruw celebrates with Mike Mordecai, Terry Pendleton, and Rafael Belliard as the Braves win Game 5 of the National League Championship Series and begin their comeback against the St. Louis Cardinals.

In the Division Series against the Los Angeles Dodgers, Andruw barely played. The Braves swept the three-game series and advanced to meet the St. Louis Cardinals. The Cards dropped the opening game of the best-of-seven series, then came back to win the next three games. The Braves blew out St. Louis in Games 5 and 6, then squeezed out a heart-stopping victory in Game 7 to win the National League pennant.

Andruw got to start two of the playoff games in left field. He did well, and even hit a home run. At 19, he became the youngest player ever to hit a homer in postseason play. This was just a hint of the incredible things to come.

Andruw's World

chapter 4

"We've been looking for a hero for a long time, and we finally found one."
— JOBI HENRIQUES, CURAÇAO TOURISM OFFICIAL

The people of Curaçao prepared for the 1996 World Series as if for a festival. For the first time ever, one of their own would be a part of baseball's ultimate event. Huge screens were set up in sports stadiums so thousands could watch the games. And Andruw's parents flew up to New York to watch him in person.

As the experts analyzed the meeting between the Braves and New York Yankees, they felt that the Yanks had little hope of winning. The only chance New York had was to keep Atlanta's power hitters at bay. Most of

Did You Know?

Andruw became the youngest player ever to start a World Series game. The previous record was held by Mickey Mantle.

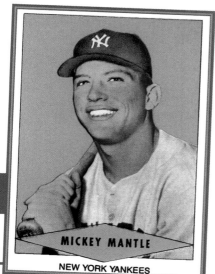

MICKEY MANTLE
NEW YORK YANKEES

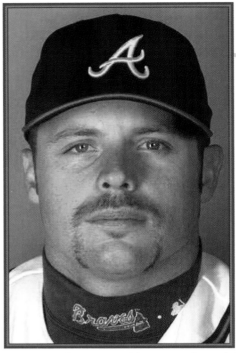

Slugger Ryan Klesko, who was benched in favor of Andruw for Game 1 of the 1996 World Series.

the Braves' slugging took place from the left side. Lefties Ryan Klesko and Fred McGriff had combined for 62 homers, and switch-hitting Chipper Jones did most of his damage from that side, too. The best way to defend against left-handed power is with left-handed pitching. The Yankees had three left-handed starters, Andy Pettitte, Jimmy Key, and Kenny Rogers.

This was bad news for the Braves, but good news for Andruw, who is right handed. Despite his late-season slump, it looked like he would get plenty of playing time. Game 1 took place in Yankee Stadium, which has the most spacious left field in all of baseball. Normally, Klesko played left. But Bobby Cox feared he would not be able to cover so much territory, so he asked Andruw to start. It had been almost 20 years since a teenager had appeared in a World Series game, and Andruw was starting the opener!

New York started Pettitte, a 21-game winner. He mowed down the first three Braves to open the game, then struck out McGriff to start the second inning. He seemed to be sailing right along when Andruw came to the plate with two down and Javier Lopez, who had poked a single, standing on first base. Andruw looked as calm as he had a few months earlier in Class-A Durham. He even appeared to have a little smile on his face. You would never know from his expression that this was the biggest at bat of his young life.

Pettitte, the big, intense left-hander, was not smiling. He wanted to end the inning right then and there. Annoyed at Andruw's nonchalance, he decided to throw a cut fastball inside to intimidate the young hitter. Andruw recognized the pitch instantly. He knew it was coming in hard, and that it was spinning toward his fists. He whipped his bat around in a mighty uppercut and caught Pettitte's pitch perfectly. The ball rose toward left field in a majestic arc before dropping over the fence for a two-run homer.

Andruw watches the ball rise toward the left-field stands. His second-inning homer against the Yankees made him the youngest player ever to hit a round-tripper in World Series play. As Andruw adds more muscle to his 6 foot 1 inch, 210 pound frame, his homers should go up.

An inning after his first blast, Andruw admires his second consecutive World Series home run.

In the Braves' dugout, a wild scene was taking place. In Curaçao, it was even wilder. In the Yankee dugout, manager Joe Torre and pitching coach Mel Stottlemyre sensed they were in for a long night. The last guy on the Braves they thought would hurt them was Andruw Jones. On the mound, Pettitte was furious with himself.

An inning later, Pettitte was yanked out of the game after allowing the Braves to score three more times. His reliever, Brian Boehringer, now had to deal with Andruw. Andruw settled into the batter's box, squinted at Boehringer, and smiled. Moments later, he was trotting around the bases again. Andruw had hit another bomb to left field, and the Braves had three more runs on the board for a commanding 8–0 lead. Andruw added a third hit and another run later in the game, and the Braves went on to win, 12–1.

Atlanta ace Greg Maddux, whose brilliant pitching in Game 2 gave the Braves a 2-0 series lead.

The Braves took the second game in New York, as Greg Maddux defeated Jimmy Key, 4–0. Back in Atlanta, Andruw was in the starting lineup for the third straight game, despite the fact that David Cone, a right hander, was on the mound for New York. The Yankees managed a 5–2 win, and Andruw went hitless. But in Game 4, the young man had a huge game. Five times he came to the plate, and he reached base all but once. Thanks to Andruw, Atlanta took a 6–3 lead into the eighth inning, and their ace relief pitcher, Mark Wohlers, was on the mound.

In the history of the World Series, only three teams had come back from a 3–1 deficit in games to win it all. If Wohlers could get the final six outs, Andruw knew the Braves were likely to be champions again. From his position in left field, he watched as the Yankees scratched out a couple of hits. Then backup catcher Jim Leyritz came to the plate. Andruw did not expect the ball to be hit his way. Wohlers could hit 100 miles (160 kilometers)

Did You Know?

Only one other player in history—Gene Tenace of the 1972 Oakland A's—has hit home runs in his first two World Series at bats.

Andruw gives it everything he has got but cannot reach Jim Leyritz's home run.

per hour on the radar gun, and only a couple of right-handed hitters in all of baseball were quick enough to "pull" the ball to left against him.

Andruw grew excited as Wohlers got two quick strikes on Leyritz. Then, for some reason, Wohlers threw a slow curve that broke right over the plate. Leyritz was fooled by the pitch's slow speed, but stayed back long enough to get good wood on the ball and send it on a high arc toward Andruw. He drifted back to the fence and got ready to jump, but the ball just kept going and going. Suddenly it was 6–6. The Atlanta crowd was stunned. The Braves were stunned.

Neither team scored in the ninth inning. In the 10th, pitcher Steve Avery allowed the Yankees to load the bases. A walk and an error led to two runs. The Braves failed to score in their half of the inning and lost,

8–6. What had once seemed like a certain championship for the Braves was now slipping away.

In Game 5, Pettitte came back for the Yankees and avenged the loss he had suffered in New York with a 1–0 shutout. In Game 6, the Yankees put three runs on the board early and the Braves just could not catch up. Andruw reached base four times in the final two games, but the middle of the Atlanta batting order failed to hit. New York won the game by a score of 3–2 to complete a remarkable comeback and win the World Series.

Andruw was extremely disappointed, but also very proud of his performance. His two home runs, six RBIs, and .400 batting average was the best hitting performance of anyone in the World Series. When Andruw returned home for the winter, he felt even prouder. A new sign had been erected at the airport. It read, "Welcome to Curaçao, Home of Andruw Jones." There had even been a popular song written about him!

The Jones File

ANDRUW'S FAVORITE...

Sport to Play . . . . Basketball
Hobby . . . . Bike Riding
Player . . . . Ken Griffey, Jr.
"I like to see him play. Some people compare me to him."
Number 13
(The same number his dad wore)
Thing About Being a Baseball Player . . . . . Traveling, seeing new places, and meeting new people
Saying . . . . . . "The more you learn, the better you become."

The thing that pleased Andruw most was seeing how many kids were playing baseball in his country. There is not much to do on the island for a bored teenager, and drug abuse was becoming a major concern for the government. Andruw had inspired many boys to rediscover baseball, and that felt really, really good.

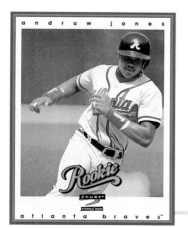

Collectors went scrambling for Andruw's rookie cards after the 1996 World Series.

Thunder from the Bench

chapter 5

"He's good. He knows he's good. And he knows everybody knows he's good."

— CHIPPER JONES

Andruw began 1997 unsure of his role with the team. Obviously, he had proved that he could perform under pressure. And no one questioned his skills. But the Braves had some great outfielders in training camp, and he did not see where he fit in. Andruw made the mistake most young players make in this situation: He tried to do too much and ended up doing nothing. He struggled to keep his average above .200, and made bad plays in the field. The game that had once come so easily to Andruw suddenly seemed very hard.

When you're hot, you're hot. In 1997, more than 20 different baseball cards of Andruw were printed.

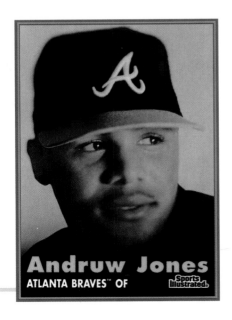

Andruw Jones
ATLANTA BRAVES™ OF
Sports Illustrated

Not many teenagers make the cover of BASEBALL DIGEST, the oldest monthly baseball magazine there is.

As Opening Day approached, Andruw wondered whether he would even make the team. He did not like the idea of spending another season in the minor leagues. A week before the season began, Andruw got a lucky break. The Braves traded outfielders Marquis Grissom and Dave Justice to the Cleveland Indians for star center fielder Kenny Lofton. Although Andruw wanted to play center field, he was happy that there was one less outfielder competing for a spot. When the Braves left spring training, Andruw was on the team.

Unfortunately, he was also on the bench. Michael Tucker, who had come to the team that spring from the Kansas City Royals, won the right-field job. With Lofton in center field and Ryan Klesko in left field, Andruw had a hard time breaking into the starting lineup. Bobby Cox considered sending Andruw to the minors, where he could play every day. But in the end he decided to keep him in the majors. Cox believed that Andruw was the kind of person who could watch and learn even when he was not playing. The Braves' manager tried to use him almost every day—as a pinch-hitter, pinch-runner, or defensive replacement—so he would always be thinking about what was going on out on the field.

"I believe we're in the midst of seeing something really special."

BOBBY COX,
BRAVES' MANAGER

Andruw rewarded Cox's confidence in him by coming through with big plays. In the 10th inning of an early-season game against the San Diego Padres, Andruw came in against the league's top closer, Trevor Hoffman, and smashed a pinch-hit home run to win the game. When Lofton missed five weeks in June and July with a leg injury, Andruw filled in nicely in center field. By the time Lofton returned, Andruw was among the team leaders in home runs, slugging average, and steals.

During Andruw's time as a regular, National League pitchers finally got a good look at him. They found that he still could be tempted into swinging at curves that danced around the outside of the plate, and that he could be tricked into swinging at fastballs several inches above the top of the strike zone. Not even the greatest hitters can make solid contact with these pitches consistently. Andruw saw his batting average plummet more than 50 points. Once again, it was time to "adjust" to the adjustments the pitchers had made.

At first, Andruw struggled to understand what the pitchers were doing to get him out. Was there a flaw in his swing? Then it dawned on him: He was getting *himself* out! There was nothing wrong with his swing. The pitchers simply knew what he was expecting in certain situations. They gave him pitches that looked a lot like what he was expecting, but ended up being a little different. They were throwing sliders that Andruw thought were fastballs, curves he thought were change-ups, and fastballs he thought were curves. He realized that he had to study the pitchers, and start outsmarting *them*.

At an age when most young men are trying to figure out what size fries to order in the Drive-Thru, Andruw was trying to analyze what veteran pitchers like Kevin Brown, Curt Schilling, and Roger Clemens were going to throw him in do-or-die situations. The Braves were confident that Andruw would be able to do this—so confident, in fact, that they handed the center-field job to their 21-year-old star for the 1998 season.

After a slow start, Andruw rewarded the team's faith in him by going on a batting tear. The key was relaxing, keeping his mind clear, and having confidence in his abilities. Bobby Cox was thrilled with Andruw's new approach to hitting. But he was growing concerned about Andruw's play in the outfield. On several occasions during the early months of the 1998 season, Andruw's mind seemed to be somewhere else, and he botched easy plays. After these errors, Andruw would smile and try to act nonchalant. He knew he had messed up, but hoped no one else would notice.

"He's got the total package!"

**MARQUIS GRISSOM,
FORMER TEAMMATE**

Eye-popping plays like this one have some fans saying that Andruw is the best young outfielder they have ever seen.

In a July game, Andruw got a bad jump on a ball hit in front of him. Instead of sprinting to make a diving try, he jogged toward the ball and simply picked it up and threw it back to the infield. Cox decided to send a message to Andruw. The manager pulled him out of the game right then and there, and roasted him after the game. It was time for Andruw Jones to grow up, Cox told reporters. No one who loafs after balls should be allowed on the field.

Andruw got the message. No one had ever accused him of trying less than 100 percent, and he was very embarrassed. From that day on, Cox never had to say another word. Andruw finished the year strong. In fact, he won the Gold Glove for his outstanding defense. Looking back, the whole incident seems silly to Andruw. After all, the thing he enjoys most is making a great catch. "I love taking hits away from guys," he smiles, "and seeing their reaction."

Big Steps to Stardom

chapter 6

"All I want is to make it to the World Series...and win it."

—ANDRUW JONES

etween the 1998 and 1999 seasons, Andruw toured Japan with a group of major-league All-Stars. He talked with the veterans and watched how they practiced and played. He also did a lot of thinking about what he had to do to achieve the great things everyone was predicting for him. He had just gone through one full year as an everyday major leaguer, and it had been a success. But the Braves had lost again in the playoffs, this time to the San Diego Padres. Andruw had not played poorly, but he had not helped all that much, either.

Andruw wanted to be the kind of player who could inspire his team to do great things, and make the kinds of plays and get the kinds of hits that win ball games. He wanted to be the kind of player who fans, teammates, and even opponents admired. "If you are doing something, do it with pride and do it hard," he says. "If you play a sport, you've got to do it with your heart."

Andruw had a great example to follow in teammate Andres Galarraga. The "Big Cat" had joined the Braves the season before and provided leadership both on the field

*Venezuelan star Andres Galarraga, whom Andruw (right) admired
as a boy, became his friend and teammate in 1998.*

and in the clubhouse. Whenever the team needed a hit, Galarraga seemed to get it, and nothing got past him in the field. More important, if a player was injured, in a slump, or had just made a bad play, the big first baseman was right there with a toothy smile and words of encouragement. Andruw was thrilled to be on the same team as Galarraga. A native of Venezuela, he was a hero to baseball fans throughout nearby Curaçao.

Andruw decided the first thing he needed to do was work on his body. There had been times in 1998 when he knew exactly what kind of pitch was coming, but had failed to drive the ball. This he attributed to a lack of strength. So during the off-season, he started a conditioning program designed to turn his willowy frame into solid rock.

When Andruw arrived at spring training, the Braves were pleased to see him in such terrific shape. They told him 1999 would be his year—they were counting on it. The team's new hitting coach, Don Baylor, told Andruw that for this to happen, he would have to make some changes in his swing. It was great that he was bigger and stronger, said Baylor, but there were a lot of big, strong guys in baseball who would love to have Andruw's lightning-quick wrists. Why wasn't he using them more?

Andruw had no answer. Baylor explained that having quick, powerful wrists meant that Andruw could wait an instant longer before starting his swing. During that instant, he could get a better idea of where a pitch was headed and what it might do. Baylor promised Andruw that if he cut down on his swing and used his wrists more, he would not only get more walks and less strikeouts, but pitchers would start giving him better pitches to hit.

Thanks to his off-season work, the advice of Baylor, and the inspiration of Galarraga, Andruw took a major step forward in 1999. He played in every game and improved in almost every offensive category. Andruw was second on the team in hits, homers, and walks, and third in doubles, RBIs, and stolen bases. For the second-straight year, he led National League outfielders in putouts and earned a Gold Glove.

Baseball insiders looked beyond the stats and saw other important changes in Andruw. He was learning how to "control" his at bats. By refusing to swing at breaking balls with less than two strikes, he forced pitchers to give him at least one good pitch to hit every time he was up. Also, he got better against a pitcher the more times he

Did You Know?

In the spring of 1999, the Braves got terrible news. Andres Galarraga had cancer. The "Big Cat" missed the entire season while undergoing treatment, and many feared his career was over. In 2000, Galarraga beat the odds and returned to the field, slamming a dramatic home run in his first game back with the Braves.

faced him. And he hit very well in the late innings, when the pressure was greatest.

On the bases, Andruw was fantastic. He regularly went from first to third on singles, and from first to home on doubles. In the field, he was better than ever, making diving plays and incredible running catches to save the Atlanta pitching staff dozens of runs.

Atlanta's "other" Jones, Chipper, may have won the National League's Most Valuable Player Award in 1999, but in many ways Andruw was just as valuable. Because Bobby Cox could rely on him day after day after day, the manager had the confidence to tinker with the rest of his lineup when injuries and illness ended the seasons of Galarraga, catcher Javier Lopez, and speedster Otis Nixon. The Braves won their division again, and this time made it back to the World Series.

Although Andruw is not among the league leaders in steals, he is one of baseball's best base runners. He rarely misses an opportunity to take an extra base, and is almost never thrown out.

What could have been a perfect finish to a beautiful season, however, ended as a big disappointment. Facing the New York Yankees again, the Braves struggled against New York's pitchers. Even Andruw, the star of the 1996 Fall Classic, could not manage more than one hit in four games. Atlanta's pitching, which seemed to be the equal of New York's, did not get the job done either. In each of the Braves' four losses, the Yankees managed to break through for one big inning.

Once again, Andruw and the Braves were on the outside looking in. Once again, he felt awful.

Love that Glove

Here's what baseball people are saying about the spectacular defense of Andruw Jones...

"You cannot hit a ball over his head. If the ball's over his head, it's out of the ballpark."
TIM MCCARVER, TWO-TIME ALL-STAR

"Defensively, he's as good as it gets.... I can't imagine how he could be any better. I really can't."
BOBBY COX, BRAVES' MANAGER

"He makes things look easier than they are."
JOHN SCHUERHOLZ, BRAVES' GM

chapter 7 # Beyond Compare

"He reminds me so much of Willie Mays. In fact, since Willie, I don't think I've seen a better defensive center fielder than Andruw."

—BOBBY COX, BRAVES' MANAGER

Ask Andruw about the 1999 World Series and he will tell you it was one of the most frustrating experiences of his young life. Ask him if he would rather forget it and he will smile and shake his head "No." During the series he got a chance to meet Willie Mays, the greatest all-around center fielder ever. Andruw actually got goose bumps talking to him! He was excited to learn that Mays had followed a similar path to stardom. Like Andruw, he came to the majors on the strength of his natural ability. He transformed himself into a superstar by learning as much as he could about himself and his opponents. Andruw hoped the same formula would work for him.

After working closely with Andruw for four years, Bobby Cox can finally sit back, relax, and enjoy his star center fielder.

As the 2000 season wore on, it looked like he was on the right track. Once again, Andruw took major steps forward in every area. Pitches he had just missed in past seasons were now flying out of the ballpark. And it was the *pitchers* who were now desperately trying to adjust to *Andruw*. He also was starting to assert himself as a leader. When the team needed a lift, he no longer looked around for Andres or Chipper or Javy to provide it. Andruw went out and got the job done himself.

In sports, this is known as "maturity." The Braves were pleased that Andruw had taken this important step forward, especially during the early part of the season, when their clubhouse was more like a madhouse. Some stupid remarks made by John Rocker about the people of New York City had created a swirl of controversy that easily could have distracted a young player like Andruw. Not only was Andruw able to ignore this situation, he became an All-Star!

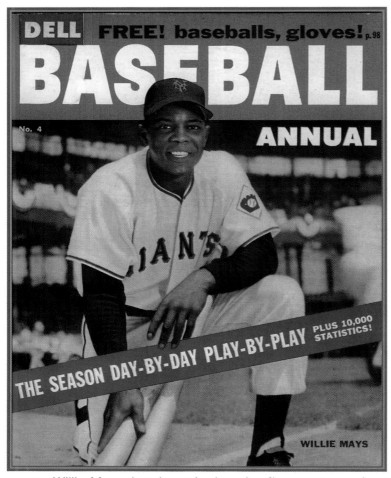

DELL FREE! baseballs, gloves! p.98

BASEBALL

No. 4

ANNUAL

THE SEASON DAY-BY-DAY PLAY-BY-PLAY PLUS 10,000 STATISTICS!

WILLIE MAYS

Willie Mays, to whom Andruw is often compared, had already won an MVP by the time he appeared on this magazine cover in 1955. Andruw's fans believe he is just a season or two away from competing for the award.

Although the ultrapopular Junior Griffey was elected to the starting lineup by the fans, a lot of baseball people believed Andruw deserved to start. At the All-Star break, he was fourth in the league in runs, fifth in hits, and sixth in total bases. Andruw did not care. He was just happy to be selected—especially because the All-Star Game was in Atlanta.

Andruw's eyes were as big as saucers as he mingled with baseball's best players, past and present. Hank Aaron, the Braves' greatest player, threw out the first ball. Dale Murphy, who won two MVPs as Atlanta's center fielder in the 1980s, was the honorary captain for the National League All-Stars. Before the game began, Andruw got a huge ovation from the hometown fans when he was introduced. As he trotted across the diamond during the introduction ceremonies, he tried to imagine the reaction of the fans back home in Curaçao.

They were going crazy, of course. But that was nothing compared to the wildness that followed Andruw's first at bat, in the fifth inning. Facing Oakland closer Jason Isringhausen—who has one of the best curveballs in the majors—Andruw socked a single to center that scored Gary Sheffield.

Hey, 19!

Becoming an "impact player" as a 19-year-old put Andruw in some very impressive company. Here are some of history's greatest teen stars. Each was 19 or younger when he made headlines on the major-league level.

PLAYER	YEAR	TEAM	KEY STAT	CAREER ACHIEVEMENT
Bert Blyleven	1970	Twins	Won 10 for AL West champs	287 career victories
Ty Cobb	1906	Tigers	Batted .316 with 23 SBs	.367 career average
Tony Conigliaro	1964	Red Sox	Hit .290 with 24 HRs	Youngest HR champ at 20
Bob Feller	1938	Indians	Led AL in strikeouts	6-time AL victory leader
Dwight Gooden	1984	Mets	Led NL in strikeouts	2000+ career strikeouts
Ken Griffey, Jr.	1989	Mariners	16 HRs & 16 SBs	4-time HR champ
Catfish Hunter	1965	A's	Pitched 2 shutouts in 20 starts	8-time All-Star
Andruw Jones	1996	Braves	2 HRs in 1st World Series game	Gold Glove winner & All-Star
Fred Lindstrom	1924	Giants	Hit .333 in World Series	.311 career average
Mickey Mantle	1951	Yankees	Won RF job for AL champs	536 career HRs
Mel Ott	1928	Giants	.322 & 18 HRs	511 career HRs
Ivan Rodriguez	1991	Rangers	Hit .264 as everyday catcher	Won 1999 AL MVP
Amos Rusie	1890	Giants	Led NL in strikeouts	5-time 30-game winner
John Ward	1879	Grays*	Led NL in wins & strikeouts	Hall of Famer
Robin Yount	1975	Brewers	149 hits & 12 SBs	2-time AL MVP

* FRANCHISE FOLDED IN 1886

When historians look back on this game, they probably will not remember Andruw's single. What they will remember is that he was one of 26 first-time All-Stars. It was truly a "changing of the guard," as the game's newest stars staked their claim on baseball's future. Who among these young All-Stars will go on to achieve greatness? No one can say.

One thing, however, is certain. Players like Andruw Jones do not come along very often. When they do, they often find themselves trying to live up to impossible expectations. That can

Did You Know?

When Andruw smiles in tense situations, many fans feel he is not taking the game seriously. Andruw's response? "People take it the wrong way at time....I'm just having fun. I take the game seriously, but it's fun to me. How can you not have fun playing a game you love?"

When you make your living with your glove, it is nice to know that you are one of the best.

be a dangerous thing, for in baseball a young player occasionally has to take a step backward in order to make a great leap forward. Many young "phenoms" fight against this process and suffer. A few, like Andruw, embrace this strange part of baseball. Because of this, there may be no limit to how good he can be.

If Andruw does develop into a superstar, it is hard to say which great center fielder he will most resemble. He is similar to Willie Mays in many respects, but is less explosive on the basepaths and at the plate. He is a more refined hitter and fielder than Mickey

major-league stats

Year	Hits	2B	3B	HR	RBI	SB	AVG
1996	23	7	1	5	13	3	.217
1997	92	18	1	18	70	20	.231
1998	158	33	8	31	90	27	.271
1999	163	35	5	26	84	24	.275
2000	199	36	6	36	104	21	.313
Total	**635**	**129**	**21**	**116**	**361**	**95**	**.272**

major-league highlights

Youngest Player to Hit Postseason Home Run	1996
Second Player to Hit Home Runs in First Two World Series At Bats	1996
Led National League in Putouts and Total Chances	1998–2000
Gold Glove Winner	1998–2000
National League All-Star	2000

Mantle, but does not have his raw power. Some say Joe DiMaggio is the old-timer Andruw most resembles, although fans of the "Yankee Clipper" are quick to point out that Andruw will never be as smooth or disciplined a hitter.

Andruw, of course, is honored to be mentioned in the same breath as these legends, but insists the fans are wasting their time. Andruw Jones is Andruw Jones, and not even *he* knows how good he will one day be. "I want to be myself," he says. "I just try to play like myself and do the best I can. I don't worry about comparisons.... I don't worry about money, I don't worry about publicity, I don't worry about any of that stuff."

Barry Bonds, winner of eight Gold Gloves, thinks Andruw will one day surpass him.

Atlanta fans hope National League rivals will be trying to "keep up with the Joneses" for many years to come.

Opponents of the Braves worry about Andruw. Those who play Atlanta several times a year insist that they can actually see improvements in Andruw's game from one series to the next. Barry Bonds, one of the greatest left fielders of all time, says Andruw could one day be the best center fielder ever. His fellow Braves also are in awe of him. Greg Maddux, one of the smartest pitchers in history, is impressed by how well Andruw understands the game. Chipper Jones, the 1999 National League MVP, claims Andruw looks like he "knows something about baseball that no one else does."

What is the next step for Andruw? As he gains more knowledge and experience, he must use it every time he steps into the batter's box, or leads off a base, or positions himself in the outfield. That is when fans will begin to see the things that make a very good player into a Hall of Famer.

What does Andruw see when he looks into his crystal ball? He is determined to keep getting better, keep having fun, and keep meeting the expectations his fans and fellow players have for him. "Do you know what I want?" he asks. "I want one day, when I retire, for people to say, 'There goes Andruw Jones. He's the best center fielder I've ever seen.'"

Andruw may be "The Man" when he is in uniform, but away from the ballpark he is still just a kid at heart.

baseball's new wave

Index